Travis A. Branch

Maiden's Adventure

Travis A. Branch

Maiden's Adventure

ISBN/EAN: 9783337341893

Printed in Europe, USA, Canada, Australia, Japan

Cover: Foto ©Andreas Hilbeck / pixelio.de

More available books at **www.hansebooks.com**

A COMEDY DRAMA

IN SIX ACTS.

Maiden's Adventure.

SCENE ON THE UPPER JAMES.

———

By TRAVIS ALBERT BRANCH.

———

—◄●►— ⸺

RICHMOND:
TAYLOR & DALTON, PRINTERS.
1893.

MAIDEN'S ADVENTURE.

CAST OF CHARACTERS.

Victor Herndon.................................A Young Lawyer
Dr. Joshua Hill.........................An Old (Bachelor) Uncle
John Hill....................................Nephew of Joshua Hill
Charles Crane.,.....................................A Gambler
Policeman......................................——— ———
Sheriff...——— ———
Paul..A Negro Servant
Silas..A Negro Servant
Myra Grainer.........................Niece of Joshua Hill
Florence Hill...........................Niece of Joshua Hill
Mrs. Brooks.........................Boarding Mistress
Miss Kate.................................An Old Maid
Diana....................................A Servant to Myra
Catherine............................A Servant to Florence
Puss........................A Servant at Boarding-House
Lucy..................................Servant to Victor
Bill Robertson and Others.

MAIDEN'S ADVENTURE.

ACT ONE.

Scene I.—Library at West View Villa. [Enter John Hill.]

JOHN—I guess that stupid old uncle of mine is satisfied, he has brought Richard Gramer's child here to inherit his fortune; he has forsworn 'tis true. I have heard him sware that Richard Gramer, his wife, nor child should never cross his threshold. Florence, my cousin, he abhors, and I, his preferred heir, shall not be cut off from my uncle's fortune by Richard Gramer's child. Not enough of her blood runs in my veins for me to be merciful if she comes between me and Joshua Hill's million, for that million I must and will have. Here comes the old man now. [Enter Joshua.]

JOSHUA—Halloo! Halloo! What brings you so early, are you sick? Do you feel like you look? Come my boy and let me feel your pulse, I am sure you must be sick from the way you look.

JOHN—I am sorry, uncle, my looks deceive you. I am feeling quite well, thank you. I am glad to see you looking so well.

JOSHUA—O, John, I am glad you are considered a judge, do you think I am looking well?

JOHN—Yes; you are almost as large as a hogshead.

JOSHUA—Well, you know I have the dyspepsia and am drinking beer for a remedy, and it is an excellent one, it has a stretching capacity, a strong desire to extend my corporation.   '

JOHN—And it seems that its desire has been accomplished, for you are immense.

JOSHUA—Well, my boy, it does seem so; I suppose, John, you will try a dose of my medicine, won't you? [Summons a servant.]

JOHN—Yes; I'll take a glass, thank you.

JOSHUA—Look here, John, I believe your girl has bounced you, you look like you have lost your marbles, what is the matter with you?

JOHN—I hav'nt given anyone the chance. [Enter Paul.]

PAUL—Sarvant, Massa Josh; sarvant, Mass John; sarvant, sar?

JOSHUA—Halloo, you are too polite to be honest, you black monkey, you; bring me some beer in short notice.   ·

PAUL—[Aside] Massa John looks like de—[aloud, he sings] de last rose of summer.

JOSHUA—I say, John—Oh, hush that fuss, hush that fuss. [Paul still sings.]

JOHN—I don't know which is making the most fuss, you or he. Is that the way you rear your servants, to go yelling about the house in that manner.

JOSHUA—Why, that negro sings delightfully; I taught him how to sing.

JOHN—[Aside.] I thought so. [Enters Paul, still singing.]

JOSHUA—What are you yelling about here for? [Paul stops suddenly.] I'll make you drink this glass of beer, you black scoundrel. [Paul trembles and falls on his knees. Josh makes him drink the beer. Paul appears he doesn't like it, and laughs at him behind his back. Josh drinks the remaining glass and sits the other on the table. John picks it up and starts to drink.]

JOSHUA—Hold on, John, don't drink the glass, I'll have you some brought. [To Paul.] Bring me some more beer, steam-piano, for you can make as much fuss as two. [Exit Paul.] I say, John, don't you think that boy can sing?

JOHN—Yes; I think he has accomplished more of the art than his master. [John still remaining.]

JOSHUA—Well, that is how you are raised. You may be a judge of good looks, but not of good singing. [Enters Paul, bearing the beer.]

PAUL—Here you is, Massa. [Josh takes one, hands it to John; Paul drinks the rest while he is so doing.]

JOSHUA—John, this is the best beer in America; sometimes I wish I were a Dutchman. This— [He sees Paul drinking the other glass of beer, stoops down, watches him drink. Paul looks first at the bottom of the glass and then spies his master; he then backs out under his searching gaze.] Well,

George, that negro beats all I have ever seen, he
will have enough of drinking when he gets hold of
that bottle of wine. I say, John, have you seen
your little counsin?

JOHN—No, I have not.

JOSHUA—Well, I'll have her summoned.

JOHN—No, don't bother yourself; I don't care to
see her.

JOSHUA—Well, my dear boy, you never saw a
lovelier creature in your life, or a sweeter one.

JOHN—Yes, very sweet, indeed; something like
her mother. You'll spend your money to educate
her and then she will marry some vagabond.

JOSHUA—Come, sir, how dare you speak of your
aunt and child in that manner? She had but one
fault; she loved too passionately one who was not
worthy of her affections. She disobeyed my wishes,
and in a fit of madness I swore she should never
cross my threshold. She died in want without my
knowledge, and for the sin of that oath I'll make
amends to her daughter. Oh, Mary, Mary, had I
not sworn that oath. [Tears steal down his
cheeks.]

JOHN—Uncle Josh will you excuse me?

JOSHUA—O, certainly, certainly, but one thing
first young man, don't ever allude to your aunt in
my presence again, and shame for this time. Now
go and drown your troubles in some sport that
would suit you best.

JOHN—Thank you, uncle, I'll drown my troubles
soon enough. [Aside.] In a manner you little expect.

JOSHUA—[Bows low.] Certainly, ha! ha! ha! by jolly, the boy is mad; he thinks his financial neck is broken, an arrogant young dude. He is very much like his mother, judging from the amount of his insolence. Hoot! hoot! I am getting mad myself. [Summons Paul.] I generally drown my troubles with a big drink. [Enter Paul.] Some wine. [He begins to pout and knocks things around generally.]

PAUL—All right massa. [Aside.] I is guine get another drink. Begins to sing. [Exit Paul.]

JOSHUA—Angels and ministers of grace defend us, if I don't kill that negro. [Grabs up the broom and knocks him down as he enters. Paul spills the wine on the floor and licks it up. As he is lying on the floor, Josh looks at him a moment or two, then beats him off the stage. He sits in front of the audience a few moments breathing very hard.] Oh, that negro, he will be the death of me, confound him; he is so fond of licking, I'll get Mason to lick him, and that decent, but I'll fix him and Silas, too, the scamps; they have stolen a bottle of wine that I put pepper in; they will think it was made of pepper instead of grapes, and that the devil was the manufacturer of it, for I am going to play ghost and scare them like the devil. He dresses like a ghost. [Exit Josh.]

Scene II.—Darkies cabin. [Enters Josh.]

JOSHUA—Just in time, here they come. Where must I get? Right behind this barrel. [Secretes.] Oh, you scamps, I'll make you think the devil is boss in this shanty. [Enters Paul and Silas.]

PAUL—Ha! ha! ha! Silas, massa guine think he drinked dis wine, but he guine think wrong dis time, ain't he doe?

SILAS—Yes, he is; nigger love wine same as white folks. [Paul starts to drink.] Look here, look here nigger, fo you mess wid dat wine, half longs to dis nigger. [Grabs Paul by the arm.]

PAUL—Take here, I is guine give you half. O, take here, take here; I is guine drink. [He drinks, turns his head, and hands the bottle to Silas; he drinks, and sets the bottle down very easy; both go through as many foolish actions as necessary; then the ghost appears, blows out the light, and scares them almost to death. Exit both]

[Josh bursts into a fit of laughter. Exit Josh.]

DIANA—[Enter Diana bearing a sword, followed by Paul and Silas] Whar did you see de debil. I'll make him know his place. . Whar is he?

PAUL—Right ober dar, mammy—worp! [He starts back.]

DIANA—Whar? [She gets frightened.]

SILAS—Mammy, he is big as old Sal mule.

DIANA—Ah! chillon, 'tis dat good ole father of valls come to tell valls to 'pent and 'pent speedily. I tell you, chillon, you had better 'pent, for the time is coming when you can't, can't 'pent.

PAUL—Mammy, if dat is father, he is done turned to de debil, for he sartinly had horns.

DIANA—You talk fool, nigger. Your father was

a 'Siple, and come to tell yall ob de sin yall been done. You better 'pent and 'pent speedy, 'cause you guine be dam and dam 'turnaly. What's dis here? Ah, you black sons of Ham; been stealing massa's wine. You know you is; you know you is. Hush! hush! I is guine beat you. [She looks at the bottle.] Oh! I is got such a pain. 'Postle Paul said must take some for stomach sake. [Paul and Silas look at her and nearly break their sides laughing. She drinks.] Murder! murder! fire! fire! Oh! my stomach, my stomach! Water, water! [Starts to look for water. Enter ghost. She falls upon the floor and tries to swim off. Paul sticks his head in the barrel. Silas makes an effort to escape through the private-box, turns, and tries to pass the ghost, but he catches him by the hair, then lets him go.] Scene closes.

Scene III.—Library in the same.

JOSHUA—[Alone.] Ha! ha! ha!—oh, my side. By bloods, if I haven't had some fun this night. I don't want a cent. [He rings for Diana. Enter Diana.] Halloo, old mammy, I thought you were in the fairy land.

DIANA—No, massa, not yet, but I seed death dis night—oh, my stomach.

JOSHUA—Well, what did he say?

DIANA—Ah, massa, he say, "Diana, Diana, time don't 'long"—massa, he fill me wid fire and smite me to de floor. Ah, massa, I hears dat voice calling dis old nigger; Diana, Diana, ah, 'taint guine be long. He guine take dis old black soul, den I is guine sing. [Starts humming a negro tune and patting her foot; then shouts. Exit Diana, singing as she goes.]

Joshua—Well, that will do. Go summons the two young ladies. [Enter Myra; soon after, Florence.]

Myra—O, uncle, you look so happy. [She kisses him.] What makes you so happy?

Joshua—Why, because you kissed me; isn't that enough to make a fellow happy? If you would kiss some of the boys around here, you would make them so happy they would butt their brains out.

Myra—Well, uncle, I will be sure not to cause any one to commit suicide in such a horrible manner. Oh, uncle, I have been reading Poe's " Black Cat." People say no one can read it and sleep that night, and I am trying it.

Joshua—So you are trying to be brave, are you?

Myra—Yes, I would like to be a brave girl.

Joshua—That's right, my dear child; you will need all of your bravery here, I am afraid. [Enter Florence.]

Florence—Do you wish to speak with me?

Joshua—Yes, Lady Florence, if your majesty will permit.

Florence—Then be brief.

Joshua—I will, to be sure, for your company is as obnoxious to me as mine is to you; I only wish to say that I am going to the city to engage board and school for you and Myra. Have you anything to say?

FLORENCE—Nothing; only I prefer to do both alone.

JOSHUA—Ha! ha! ha! Well, I prefer you will do both together. You can go.

FLORENCE—[Aside.] I'll get even with you. [Exit Florence.]

MYRA—Uncle, she seems at enmity with us all. Pray tell me what I have done to offend her?

JOSHUA—O, never mind her; she is a little dyspeptic, that's all; she needs beer.

MYRA—Uncle, don't you think a dose of kind words would be a better remedy? I will do anything to please her.

JOSHUA—I believe you are an angel. Suppose you try it; it is an excellent remedy, but I am afraid they will be rather hard to digest.

MYRA—I'll try it this night, uncle. [Kisses him good night. Exit Myra.]

JOSHUA—If that is not an angel, I don't know who is. Just like her mother—kind-hearted, loves peace, good to everybody, and hates no one. I will be dad blamed if she don't have a tuff customer to deal with, for that gal is the devil. [Exit Josh.]

Scene IV.—Florence's room. [Myra taps gently at the door.]

FLORENCE—Things have come to a pretty pass, that I have got to board where he sees fit, and with that asylum girl, that I may be mortified as often as possible by her ignorance. Claiming kin with me. I don't believe she is Aunt Myra's child. [Myra taps.] Come in. [Enter Myra.] I presume you have missed your way.

Myra—No, cousinFlorence; I wish to speak to you. Will you permit me?

Florence—No, I wish to confer with no one. I am in no mood for communication. Please leave my room.

Myra—May I not speak one word with you?

Florence—No, not a syllable; you have already said too much, and hereafter, when you address me, let it be Miss Florence or nothing. Now go.

Myra—Then I am not your cousin?

Florence—No, not a drop of your blood runs in my veins. Richard Gramer, your father, died a drunkard in the streets of Charleston, and your mother, a miserable pauper. [Enters Diana.]

Myra—Florence Hill, it's a *lie.* [She screams and falls in Diana's arms. Curtain falls while Diana is shaking her fist at Florence.]

ACT TWO.

Scene I.—Joshua Hill in city; meets Victor Herndon.

JOSHUA—Helloo, helloo, how much is the stakes?

VICTOR—Helloo, Doctor, you are an early bird. What brings you to town so early? [Shake hands.]

JOSHUA—Business, my boy, business; and I want to see some of my old friends.

VICTOR—Well, I hope you won't have much trouble in finding them.

JOSHUA—Well, I hope so, too. By the way, you are just the fellow I want to see. I tell you, Vic., [slaps him on the shoulder] I have the sweetest little gal at home you ever saw, and, I tell you, she is as pretty as a picture.

VICTOR—Where did you find such a beautiful creature?

JOSHUA—Victor, I have been an ungrateful dog. She is my sister's child, who died a year ago, and I have just brought her home, and Florence, my soul, is furious.

VICTOR—Doctor, I didn't know your sister had a child. How old is she?

JOSHUA—O, she is sixteen, and just from school, and as coy as a mouse.

VICTOR—O, that is a charming age, and I would be more than pleased to meet her.

JOSHUA—Well, I guess you can if you try. You will always find her under old Joshua's roof, and there, Vic, you are always welcome. I say, Vic, the early bird catches the worm. Let's have a drink. [Enter bar; scene opens.] How is business, my boy?

VICTOR—Business is brisk—very brisk. 1 have several cases of breach of promise on hand.

JOSHUA—Give us a julep. [To bar-keeper.] Girls are numerous, and as sharp as briars, and you had better mind how you court, boy. I say, I have a good one on your profession.

VICTOR—You have? Let's hear it.

JOSHUA—What is the difference between a soldier and a lawyer? Come, now; summon your wits. Hold on; let's drink first. [They drink.]

VICTOR—What is the difference between a lawyer and a soldier? Well, the only difference I can see is this: A lawyer fights with his tongue and a soldier with implements of war.

JOSHUA—Pretty good; but you are wrong. You are off the track. [Slaps him on the shoulders.]

VICTOR—Well, I'll give it up. I am not apt on problems, I'll admit.

JOSHUA—Well, you see a soldier charges upon his *enemy's* breast-work, and a lawyer upon his *friend's* pocket-book. Ha! ha! ha! That's so; isn't it, old boy? [Slaps him on the shoulder.]

VICTOR—[Aside.] If I don't leave him, he will

kill me. Doctor, that is brilliant. Let's have a julep. [To bar-keeper.] Well, we'll take another, and I must leave you.

JOSHUA—But look here—by the way, where can I find a first-class boarding-house? I want to send those gals to school in town.

VICTOR—Why, yes, there is Mrs. Brooks, 417 S. Fourth street. First-class house, fine lady, and she's a widow.

JOSHUA—Capital; let's drink on that. [He slaps at him, Victor steps aside, and Josh falls on his hands and knees.]

VICTOR—Helloo, let me pick you up.

JOSHUA—Well, I believe I need your assistance. [A boy steps into the bar, sticks him with a pin, then runs out. He jumps up in a second.] Who did that?

VICTOR—Didn't you see the boy as he ran out?

JOSHUA—No; dad blame his buttons. If I had I would have given him this foot, and it's a Number ten, too. Now, we'll take that drink, and here is luck to the widow. [They drink.]

VICTOR—Well, Doctor, I must leave you; but how did you leave all at home?

JOSHUA—All at home? Why, sick. Diana has the rheumatism, old Mary the mumps, Paul and Silas have wine on the brain, Florence the devil's dyspepsia, and I—oh! [Slaps where the boy stuck him, and looks around and tries to see the place.] Where did you say that boy went?

VICTOR—Why, that boy is at home by now.

Joshua—Well, he had better stay there, too; confound him.

Victor—Doctor, I must leave you. I am in sort of a hurry. Good day. Don't forget the widow.

Joshua—Good day. I won't forget her, you bet. [Aside.] That's a fine boy. He is in love with that gal now. I can see it in his eye. Well, go on; I don't care. But won't Florence play the devil? I say, neighbor, [to bar-keeper] it's a long time between drinks. Let's have another. Come on, you'll drink with me, won't you?

B. K.—Oh, yes; I never refuse to drink with a fine-looking fellow like you.

Joshua—Good! Give us your hand, Smith, Brown, or Jones.

B. K.—You are mistaken in the name, sir. Washington Marion Henry Lee is my name.

Joshua—Old Vet.—old soldier. Well, I haven't seen you since the war. I say, Washington Marion Henry Lee, we will drink for old acquaintance sake. You remember, Lee, when we fought side by side at the battle of Bunker Hill, when we made the "red coats" drink their blood, and at Yorktown, when we gave America her freedom? Oh, if I were an orator. Do you know my name?

B. K.—Well, I can't say I do.

Joshua—My name is Josiah Jonathan Joshua Hill.

B. K.—From your name, I would judge you were a D. D.

JOSHUA—No; oh, no; not so. If I am, I am in the wrong pew. No, sir; I am an M. D., sir. Well, I have lots of business to transact, so I must be off. Good day. Hold on, I guess you had better give me a bottle or two of stimulants to take with me. I don't like the blame stuff, but I reckon I had better have it.

B. K.—Doctor, that name of yours is enough to kill you; you had better have it changed.

JOSHUA—That name is all right. Give me another drink, and if it kills me, I'll die happy. [They drink.] Richard is himself again; let Hercules do as he will and I'll do the same. [He settles up, puts his bottles in his pocket, starts out, and then stops.] Now for Mrs.—Mrs.—Mrs.—where does she live?

B. K.—Where does who live? *

JOSHUA—O, you know who I mean; the widow.

B. K.—How do I know; the town is full of widows.

JOSHUA—Well, if you don't know, I will ask some one that does. [Exit Josh. *Scene II.*] Helloo, where am I? [Enter boy.] I say, Johnnie, where am I going?

JOHNNIE—To the devil, it seems to me. [Josh starts after him. He runs off. Josh runs against a policeman just entering.]

POLICEMAN—Hold up, here. What vos you mean by running against the city authority. I'll take you in.

JOSHUA—No, thanks, plenty. I say, old cub, you look like you are blooming. [Catches him by the nose.] What will you take for this blossom?

POL. I'll sell you dis stick, dat's vot I do.

JOSHUA—Well, what will you take for the stick? I'll buy that.

POL.—Look here, vot does ye mean? [Draws his pistol.]

JOSHUA—Well, do you want to sell that? I'll buy anything.

POL.—No, I vant to sell noting.

JOSHUA—Well, how would you like to take a drink?

POL.—Vas you got somet'ing mit you. [Josh hands him the bottle. He drinks.]

JOSHUA—[Aside: Oh, for some Cayenne!] I say, Mr. City Authority, tell me where Mrs.—Mrs.—Mrs.—O, confound her name—300—300—300—O, gol darn it.

POL.—[Draws his pistol.] I say, squire, another.

JOSHUA—[Looks down the barrel.] Anything in it?

POL.—Yes, it vas a full charge.

JOSHUA—All right, I'm trading this time. [Hands him the bottle, catches hold of the pistol; he refuses to give it up; pistol fires, police drops very scared, and swears he is shot, but holds to the bottle, and drinks it dry before he gets up.] I say, old squib, don't drink any more than you want.

POL.—No, dis vas goot viskey, squire. [He tries to rise, but falls several times, then rises, feels for his pistol, then points a stick at him] Another bottle, squire.

Joshua—Oh, I guess not. I hold trumps this time. Now, old stork, I want to find the widow's house.

Pol.—Darn de vidder's house. Vot does I know about der vidder's house?

Joshua—What do you know about this? [Draws the pistol.]

Pol —Dat vas all right, squire; dat vas all right; but have you got any more dat goot viskey?

Joshua—No; I've got no more for you. March, now, or I will take that blossom for a target.

[Exit policeman; Josh behind him.]

Scene II.—Mrs. Brooks' boarding-house. [Servant girl dusting. Enter Josh.]

Joshua—Is this the right place, my dearie? [Servant very scared.] By Jehosiphat! isn't she black? [Whistles.] Black as ten of spades at midnight. I say, did your daddy sell charcoal?

Servant—Sah?

Joshua—Is this a boarding-house? [Very quick.]

Servant—Yas—sar. [Very slow.]

Joshua — Well—I — want — to —see — your—mistress.

Servant—Sah? [Don't move.]

Joshua—I want to see your mistress very quick. [He jumps at her.] I want to see the lady. [She leaves the stage in double-quick time.]

Joshua—If that isn't a black gal, Ham never had one. Look, she is coming; I hear her sweet voice. [He straightens up.] Helloo, don't she sing.

[He throws in a few notes of bass. Enter Miss Kate, an old maid, singing; Josh unobserved.]

JOSHUA—Good morning, madam. Is this the lady of the house? [Miss Kate screams, and starts to run out. Josh heads her several times, then let's her go. Josh falls down in a fit of laughter. Enter Mrs. Brooks while he is in the act. He jumps up and assumes a *very* polite position.]

MRS. B.—Well, sir; good morning.

JOSHUA—Good morning, Mrs.—Madame—

MRS. B.—Mrs. Brooks is my name, sir.

JOSHUA—O, yes, madam; yes, madam; my memory is brief. You must excuse my humble position. Something came in here just now. I thought it was a bird when I first heard it, but when it went out it sounded like a pig under the fence. My, how she squealed!

MRS. B.—Why, sir; that was Miss Kate Smith, a young lady.

JOSHUA—Well, I should think so. Does she live here?

MRS. B.—Yes, she lives here.

JOSHUA—Excuse me. [Starts for his hat.]

MRS. B.—I believe you sent for me sir; did you not?

JOSHUA—Excuse me, again. You know my friend, madam?

MRS. B.—I don't think I know to whom you allude.

JOSHUA—Why, Victor Herndon. Everybody knows him. He is a fine boy. I've known him ever since he was a minute old. His father and I were boys together, and he fell in the grand cause of America's freedom.

Mrs. B.—O, yes, I know Vic, very well; but I cannot personate you. I would be obliged if you would introduce yourself.

Joshua—Pardon me, madam. I have the honor to present to you Dr. Josiah Jonathan Joshua Hill,

Mrs. B.—Dr. Hill, I presume?

Joshua—Yes, madam; Dr. Hill.

Mrs. B.—I believe you wished to see me on business?

Joshua—Yes, madam; I understood from my friend, Victor, that you kept a first-class boarding-house.

Mrs. B.—Yes, sir; that's what I try to do.

Joshua—Well, then, we'll come down to business. I have two nieces that I wish to get board for. Can you accommodate them?

Mrs. B.—I think I can, sir. When shall I look for them?

Joshua—Well, let me see; I guess they will be here Monday.

Mrs. B.—Very well; I will look for them. It is quite early. I presume you haven't breakfasted.

Joshua—No, madam; I have not.

Mrs. B.—Then excuse me, and I will have it here in a few moments. [Exit Mrs. B.]

Joshua—Nothing will I more willingly do. [He saunters around the room looking at its contents, and starts singing "Home, Sweet Home," and is interrupted by the entrance of Mrs. Brooks and servant, bearing the breakfast. The servant sets the breakfast on the table and runs out.]

MRS. B.—Doctor, here is your breakfast.

JOSHUA—Oh, thank you; thank you. I feel like I could eat a pig.

MRS. B.—Well, I hope you will enjoy it; but I am sorry you were interrupted in your song by my entrance; but I thought you would enjoy your breakfast more than your song, though I enjoyed it very much.

JOSHUA—[Steps up close to her.] Did you really enjoy it? My friend Herndon tells me you are a widow. Is that so?

MRS. B.—Yes, sir; I am a widow, of five years.

JOSHUA—[Aside: That's good.] And I am a bachelor of fifty and still on the carpet.

[Curtain falls.]

ACT THREE.

(After Nine Months' Interval.)

Scene I.—Mrs. Brooks' boarding-house. [Myra seated in the parlor. Enter Florence and absconds.]

Myra—I wonder why Vic stays so long? What can detain him? He promised to be here at five, and now it is most six. Uncle says he believes I am in love. Well, I really believe I am. How could I help loving Victor? He is so kind, noble, and manly. Victor is everything in my eyes. He says he loves me, and I believe he does. My very heart beats at the hearing of his footsteps. The hours we spend together seem blessed with smiles from heaven. Oh, I never dreamed of such happy hours! My life has been a sad one. I left West View nine months ago in tears, but I am thankful I can forgive her, though she has caused me many a tear of sorrow. Hush! That's Victor. [Runs to see.] Yes, that's he. He comes like the sun breaking through a dark cloud. I'll meet him. No, that's too childish. I'll pretend I am reading. [She gets a book. Enter Victor, creeps up behind her, and puts his hands over her eyes.]

Victor—Well, did you think I wasn't coming?

Myra—No, I didn't think that; but I wanted you to come. [Florence looks from behind the screen and frowns.]

Victor—Did you want to see me very bad?

Myra—Indeed, I did. I am always glad to see you.

Victor—Well, I am going to tell your fortune for being so sweet.

Florence—[Aside, with teeth clenched]: Sweet, is she?

Myra—Now, Victor, you don't mean *that*. I am not sweet.

Victor—I do; and you are just as lovely as you are sweet. Now, I am going to tell your fortune.

Myra—No, no, Victor; don't tell my fortune; it was told once by a gypsy, and since then I have had too much faith in fortune-telling.

Victor—What did she tell you, Myra?

Myra—One day, as I was roaming all alone in the fields around Glenmore, I met a haggard-looking woman. She said: "Miss, can I tell your fortune?" I consented. She said my life would be a dark one, full of sorrow, but yet there would be days of sunshine. Victor, I am happy when I am with you, but still I feel that there are troubles I have yet to bear.

Florence—[Aside]: I will see to your troubles.

Victor—Myra, don't speak so. You make me feel sad. I wasn't going to tell you a sad fortune. I was going to tell you a good one, and every word will be true.

MYRA—Well, you may tell it, if it is going to be so good and all true.

VICTOR—All right, I'll begin. Some one loves you and wonders if it is returned. He it is who stands before you and awaits an answer. [She bows her head.] Myra, can you not answer? Do you love me? Say yes and make me happy. [She remains silent.] Speak, Myra, or suspense will kill me. Say you love me.

[Florence listens, trembling with anger.]

MYRA—Victor, I do love you.

[Florence starts, then stops.]

VICTOR—Then, Myra, be my wife.

MYRA—Victor, are you free to ask that question?

VICTOR—Free? Yes, as a bird. Why do you ask am I free?

MYRA—Are you not engaged to my cousin?

VICTOR—No, no. I'll swear by the stars—by heaven—by everything—that I love no one but you. Myra, I am as free as the winds that blow. Come, now, be silent no longer. It is cowardly. Make me happy while it is in your power.

MYRA—Then you shall be happy. [She clasps him around the neck. He kisses her. Florence rushes from her hiding-place.]

FLORENCE—What means this, Victor Herndon? And you, you little wretch, hugging a man in this manner. Your uncle shall know of your conduct.

MYRA—Please, Florence. [Starts to beseech her.]

VICTOR—Stop, Myra; stop, Miss Hill. I am re-

sponsible for all. I presume you have the knowledge of our relationship, as you were an ear and
eye-witness of all that passed. Your language was
quite surprising.

FLORENCE—Silence, you coward. What right
have you to upbraid me, sir? Leave this room immediately.

VICTOR—You speak with authority, and I suppose I must obey, as I sought your presence. Come,
Myra, we'll walk. [They start.]

FLORENCE—No; *she* will remain.

VICTOR—May I, too, have the pleasure?

FLORENCE—No; your absence I prefer.

VICTOR—Then, Miss Hill, you must deliver your
lecture in the future; your cousin is engaged at
present. [Exit Myra and Victor.]

FLORENCE—You swore by heaven you loved her,
and I'll swear by heaven I will have my revenge.
You dog, that feed on hearts like mine, will find it
hard to digest. I'll foil you or lose my head to accomplish it. And you, Myra Gramer, shall not escape my revenge. It was your beauty that won
him, and it shall perish. I'll make you rue the day
that you were born. Vengeance! Vengeance is
sweet, and you shall know the vengeance of a
woman if these hands of mine shall dabble in blood
to accomplish it. [She sits in silence a few minutes. Enter servant and hands her a card. She
looks at it, then tears it in pieces.] Leave me; I
wish to see no one. Stay! Show him in. [Exit
servant.] I will make a tool of him to accomplish

my aim. He will serve my purpose if there is fifty thousand in it, and I'll make him believe that at Uncle Joshua's death I'll have full control of my father's fortune. I will promise to marry him, and that will be all. [Enter Charles Crane.]

CHAS.—Good morning, Miss Hill; I am sorry to see you looking so ill-composed. I expected to find you in better spirits, as this will be your last evening in our city.

FLORENCE—Thank you, Mr. Crane. You are complimentary, but I am not mad, as you supposed, but only a little vexed. These servants are so stupid. I am rather surprised to see you, as you said you never expected to come again.

CHAS.—Well, I did say so, but I was angry at the time, and, as the song goes, "Love has conquered pride and anger."

FLORENCE—But you don't mean that, Charlie. You don't love me.

CHAS.—But I do. I swear by the stars and by—

FLORENCE—Stop, stop! Swear not by the stars. If you love me swear by thy dagger or something by which you can defend a lady's honor or thine own.

CHAS.—I will swear by anything that pleases thee, that I love thee.

FLORENCE—A man must be a brave man for me to love.

CHAS.—Florence, do you doubt my bravery?

FLORENCE—No; I have no right to. But if you

were insulted by a gentleman, how would you resent it?

CHAS.—I would use this. [Draws a revolver.]

FLORENCE—[Aside: He is the man for me.]
Well, Charlie, I haven't been as kind to you as I
should have been, but I will be a better girl in the
future. I leave for West View to-morrow. You
must come to see me often. You will excuse me,
won't you, as I have to make ready for to-morrow. I will expect you soon at West View. Good
evening. [Exit Florence.]

CHAS.—She speaks well to-night. Well, there is
hope as long as life. She has a temper, but she has
fifty thousand hard cash, and it's the cash I want
worse, but I will take both rather than miss.
Well, I guess I'll go; I will see her at West View in
a few days. [Exit Charlie.]

[Enter Myra.]

MYRA—Where did I leave my book? Here it is.
Victor, I know, is the dearest old thing in the
world. I don't care if she did see him kiss me. He
has a right, and she has nothing to do with it. I
will acquaint Uncle Josh of Victor's desires as soon
as I see him, and that will make it all right. Oh!
I'm the happiest girl in the world, [enter Florence]
and I am going to be Victor's wife just the same.

FLORRNCE—Not if my name is Florence Hill, you
won't. [Myra turns around suddenly.] Myra
Gramer, I give you warning to beware of Victor
Herndon. He is only cajoling you. In the first
place, you are not his equal, and in the second he

is my betrothed, and if you don't understand that language, miss, he is my intended husband. Read that! [Hands her letter to read.]

MYRA—Oh! heaven defend me! Can this be true? [She crumbles the letter in her hand.]

FLORENCE—Promise me you will not see him again and I will forgive you.

MYRA—No, I will not. I believe it is false, and I will see him again.

FLORENCE—Then meet him again, if you will rob me of my husband, and I will rob you of your existence. Mark that! [Exit Florence.]

MYRA—[Swoons and then partly rises]: Victor, Victor, hast thou deceived me? [Scene closes.]

Scene II.—Florence seated in the grove at West View. [Enter Paul, bearing a letter from Victor.]

PAUL—Miss Florence, here is one letter for you. [She snatches the letter from him. He jumps. Paul, aside]: If dat had been Miss Myra, she'd gin me five cents, bringing a letter from Mr. Victor. [Exit Paul.]

FLORENCE—[Reads]: I hope you will forgive my unkind remarks, and that we will meet as friends in the future. [She tears it in pieces and speaks with fury]: Yes, I'll forgive you. I'll meet you as a friend in the future. A friend to your downfall. Oh, Victor Herndon, you shall pay for this. There is too much of my mother's blood flowing in my viens to be trampled upon by a man in this manner. Vengeance, vengeance! I'll have it, cost what it may. [Exit Florence. Scene closes.]

Scene III.—River bank at West View. Myra alone, looking very downcast, pinning a flower on her dress She hears Victor whistling at a distance. Her countenance brightens, then changes very sad.]

MYRA—O, he must not see me. [She secretes herself. Enter Victor.]

VICTOR—Where is she? They said she was here, and here is where she has been. She must be about here gathering flowers. I'll look for her. [Exit Victor.]

MYRA—Oh, Victor, dost thou know why I hide from thee? Did'st thou not swear that thou wert free? Can it be that you, so frank, so noble, would deceive me and add more sorrow to my lot? I am tangled amid the thorns. They pierce me on every side. I know not which way to go. My pleasures are like the March sunshine—they are soon vanished. O, Victor, if I tell thee, wilt thou take me away? I know he will. I do not believe him false. [Enter John Hill in disguise.] I will see him. [She looks around and sees the disguised figure. She screams; he grabs her and throws her in the water. He makes his escape. Enter Victor.]

VICTOR—Where is she? I heard her scream. My soul, she is drowning. [He leaps in and brings her out unconscious.] What means all this? [Curtain falls.]

ACT FOUR.

Scene I.—Rose Garden Villa, opposite side river.
Joshua alone in his library.

JOSHUA—Wonderful things are going to happen—
wonderful things. Florence actually condescended
to speak to me this morning, and positively smiled
when she said good morning, Uncle Josh. I am be-
wildered. There is something behind that smile.
Mark me, she wants a tremendous grant of some
sort. Helloo, here she comes.

FLORENCE—Good morning, uncle.

JOSHUA—Good morning, my fair niece. [She
frowns aside.]

FLORENCE—Uncle, I came to ask a favor of you.
[Diana starts to enter, but stops at the sight of
Florence.]

JOSHUA—Ah! What is it, my dear, you would
like me to do?

FLORENCE—There is a fellow in the city who has
fallen in love with me.

JOSHUA—Is that so? And you want my consent.

FLORENCE—No, I do not want your consent.
The fellow is a perfect bore to me, and he is coming
here to-day to see me, and I don't like to insult him.

[Diana claps her hands and leaves the door.] Will you relieve me of that trouble?

JOSHUA—Well, who is it? That is the question.

FLORENCE—His name is Charlie Crane. [He jumps from his seat.]

JOSHUA—Charlie Crane? Has that scoundrel the audacity to pay you attention? An infamous rascal. If he puts his foot on Rose Garden, I'll kick him from one end to the other. Hoot! I'm mad all over. [Enter Diana. Mason, the overseer.]

DIANA—Massa, Mr. Mason wants for to see you.

JOSHUA—[To Diana.] Very well; very well. [To Florence.] When do you expect him?

FLORENCE—To-day, he wrote me word.

JOSHUA—Very well, I'll see him. [Exit Josh.]

FLORENCE—[Alone]: Ha! ha! ha! From your madness I contract pleasure, and if you don't find kicking in the way, I am mistaken in the man.

Scene III.—Door of the same. [Enter Charlie Crane.]

CHAS.—Well, I'm here, and there is fifty thousand dollars here, too, if I can get it, but that's the trouble; she is a tuff customer to deal with, but that money I must have, and to get that I must have her. Well, I guess I can stand her for fifty thousand. I wonder if she is at home. [He raps.] No one here; I'll knock again. [He raps again.] This is a beautiful place. I wonder if it is her's. Well, what is her's will be mine. By Joe, I believe they are all away. I'll try it again. [Just as he knocks Josh pulls the door open. He steps back quick.] Good morning, Dr. Hill; good morning, sir; fine weather we are having; very pleasant, indeed, sir, for June. [Aside]: Helloo, he is deaf.

JOSHUA—Well, sir; if you are through with your good mornings and fine weather, you may tell me your business.

CHAS.—[Aside]: Well, George, that's hot [Aloud]: Well, sir, I came to see Miss Hill. Is she in?

JOSHUA—Yes, she is in. What is your business with her?

CHAS.—Strictly private, sir.

JOSHUA—I am her guardian, and I must know your business, or you cannot see her.

CHAS.—Your manner indicates that I am obnoxious to you. If you will show me in and inform Miss Hill that I wish to see her, by so doing you will rid yourself of my company; or, in other words, Mr. Crane awaits her presence. [Josh stands staring.] Well, what are you staring at?

JOSHUA—Nothing. That is as near as I can come at you.

CHAS.—You are very insulting, sir. What do you mean by addressing a gentleman in that manner?

JOSHUA—A gentleman! ha! ha! ha! Have you that audacity?

CHAS.—Look here, sir, I have enough of this; I am no hog.

JOSHUA—Well, there is not much difference between a hog and a Crane; they are both so mean that arsenic won't kill them. What is your occupation, I would like to know?

CHAS.—None of your business; you are too presumptuous for good luck. I'll stand no more of this; you must retract.

JOSHUA—You are a card merchant, I presume?

CHAS.—You are a lie, I presume. [Draws his revolver; Josh knocks him down; his revolver falls out of his hand.]

Scene IV.—Grove of the same. Charlie meets Florence as he is leaving.

CHAS.—I will kill that hound before the sun sets, an infernal scoundrel. [Enter Florence.]

FLORENCE—Why, Charlie, what means this? Who are you addressing in this manner? Has any one offended you?

CHAS.—Yes, that uncle of yours has offended me, and he shall die, as sure as my name is Crane.

FLORENCE—If he insulted you, why did you not kill him on the spot? Why now think of the act? You are a coward. You are not the man I thought you were, to take an insult, and not resent it.

CHAS.—A man! I am a man; and I am not a coward. I tried, and the elephant knocked me down, and I had no chance. That is why you call me a coward; but I will have my revenge, if it takes me a lifetime to accomplish it.

FLORENCE—Charlie, if he has offended you, he

has offended me, and revenge is mine, also. Listen, if you are what you pretend to be—

CHAS.—I am what I pretend to be, and what you say I will do.

FLORENCE—Joshua Hill has fifty thousand dollars of my money, and, besides, he has made no will; and, remember, his fortune is great, and he has but three heirs to inherit it; and I cannot come in possession of mine, or become your wife, until he is removed. What say you?

CHAS.—He shall be removed, and that in short notice.

FLORENCE—Don't be hasty, man. Do you not care something for your life? Have patience, and I will contrive some way by which you will not be accused. Remember, now, if you are successful, all that I have is yours; say no more. Come to-morrow to the end of the garden, and there await, beneath yon massive oak, the waving of this handkerchief, as a signal to meet me at the lower door of the west wing. Do not let yourself be seen. Stop; say not a word. Leave here as soon as possible; some one will be here anon. Go now and remember your reward if you are successful. [Exit Chas.] Go, you mad beast; you shall have the bones and I the marrow. This dagger shall strike the fatal blow. [Draws the dagger.] Ah, Herndon, thou fool, to carve thy name upon a weapon in such dangerous times. But you shall pay for your folly. This blade shall bring me the revenge I seek. There—there they are now. Could I not pierce her very heart; tear from her the last spot of beauty that has robbed me of the only one I ever loved. Could I not robe her with the afflictions of Job and the agonies of Dives. Oh, can I stay my hand from vengeance? Nature has formed you beautiful, but I will form your destiny. Victor Herndon, I offered you my love and you would not accept it; now receive my hatred in its greatest capacity.

[Enter Victor and Myra. Florence secretes.]

VICTOR—Do not be alarmed at what she says; she dare not touch you. What she said concerning me is as false as perdition is deep; I never dreamed of such things. To-morrow I will acquaint your uncle of my intentions.

FLORENCE—[Aside.] Not if I live.

MYRA—Promise me, Victor, you will not mention what I said about Florence. Please, Victor, promise. Will you?

VICTOR—Myra, I will promise. Bear no uneasiness concerning her; for if she harms a hair of your head, she shall pay for it two-fold. [Florence bounds towards them with a drawn dagger; starts to stab him, still unseen. Scene closes with a tableau.]

Scene V.—[Charlie on hand.]

CHAS.—I don't think I have been seen. Now for the signal from the west window. I am eager to strike the blow which will bring me both revenge and wealth. One stroke with this glittering blade and, Joshua Hill, you are no more, and I will see that Florence keeps her word. Helloo, there's the signal. [Exit Chas. Scene closes and he meets Florence in front of the scene.]

FLORENCE—[Very easy.] Have you been seen?

CHAS.—No; not by any one.

FLORENCE—Take this; you haven't a moment to lose. [Hands him a dagger.] Follow me, and leave the dagger where you pierce it. [Points to the name on the dagger. He reads the name.]

CHAS.—Victor Herndon. Where did you get this?

FLORENCE—Ask no questions. Do as I bid you. Follow me. [Exit both.]

Scene VI. [Charlie and Florence at the door of Joshua Hill's library; Joshua sitting with his back to the door; Florence points at him.]

FLORENCE—There, get your revenge. [Then she leaves for the adjoining room.]

[Charlie advances slowly up to the old man, slaps his hand over his mouth, and stabs him; in an instant brings him to the floor. He starts to leave, but hears approaching footsteps. [Enter Florence.]

FLORENCE—Fly! Fly for your life! He is coming. [He starts to do so, but Victor is too close upon him, and he secretes in the corner of the room. Exit Florence. Enter Victor.]

VICTOR—Helloo, what's the matter? [Steps quick.] My soul! What has happened? Is he dead? [He shakes him.] Doctor! Doctor! He

must have swooned. [He spies the dagger.] No!
Good heavens! He is murdered! Who could have
killed him? [Enter Florence as he draws the dagger from his breast..]

FLORENCE—Murder! Murder! You have killed
my uncle! You have killed my uncle! [She pre-
tends to weep, and kneels beside the prostrate
body. Enter Diana.]

DIANA—Oh, Lordy! Oh, Lordy! Done killed
Massa Josh! Poor Massa! Who did done it?
Who did done it? [She claps her hands together.
Enter Myra.]

FLORENCE—There stands the fiend who did the
deed!

VICTOR—Myra, I did not. I found him with
the dagger pierced in his heart. [He thuows the
dagger from him; Myra falls senseless on the floor;
Diana picks her up and carries her off. Victor fol-
lows; Florence left alone.]

FLORENCE—Now is your time. Lose not a
moment, or you will be seen. Fly, if you value
your life.

CHAS.—Which way shall I go?

FLORENCE—Go the way you came. [Exit Charlie. She shoves him out.] Go! I have finished
with you, and your reward you will receive hereafter, for the devil is a good paymaster. [She
turns to view the dead body. While so doing his
eyes fly open. She gives one scream, turns her
eyes from his, falls on one knee, and looks around
very scared. Curtain falls.]

ACT FIVE.

Scene I.—Cave on Victor Herndon's farm, one mile from West View. [Victor asleep, with a dim light burning; he talks in his sleep.]

VICTOR—I knew you thought I was innocent; now, Myra, I can face the world. [He awakes, and partly rises, and looks around a moment or two.] Ah! it's all a dream. Why did I awaken? I was so happy. Oh, if I could see her, and she would believe me innocent! I will see her. I will bear it no longer. Myra! Myra! I must see you to-night! Oh! my head is bursting. [Falls back on the bed.] Lucy, Lucy—not here. Myra will not believe me guilty, she knows my heart too well. O, Myra! if thou dost pronounce me guilty, I will live no longer; this night my spirit shall accompany the spirit of the slain! [He pulls out a bottle of poison.] This will I drink! Hush! what's that? Hasty footsteps. [He hides the bottle; enter Lucy, bearing a waiter.] Lucy, is that you?

LUCY—Yes, Massa; 'tis me. Eat your supper

now. I is got some good pan-cakes for you, and some good news, arter you eat.

VICTOR—What news, Lucy? What news? Speak, quick! I must hear!

LUCY—De 'tectives done took de train dis eben, and if you want to see Miss Myra, I think you kin, for Diana says she walks in de grove by herself 'most ebery night, and de moon is done ris now.

VICTOR—Lucy, hand me my cloak. [She hands it to him.] Thank you, good Lucy; take this. [He hands her some money.] And if I never re turn, good-bye. You have cared for me; you shall be rewarded, if I live or die.

LUCY—Massa, don't say dat, for I is only done my duty.

VICTOR—Say no more, Lucy—farewell. [Exit Victor.

LUCY—I ain't guine say good-bye, for God ain't guine punish de innocent for de guilty, and I is guine follow Massa Victor wid dis here knife. [Draws a dagger.] And if anybody do trouble old mistress'es son, he is guine feel dis point. I'll show folks how old Lucy can carve. Old massa is dead and old mistess is dead, and dis here boy is all dat I know of, and when he dies I had just live die as not, so I is guine follow him. Yonder he is, walking long dar just like he is guine walk in his grave. Poor massa. Go on; I is guine follow you. [Exit Lucy.]

Scene II.—Grove at West View. [Enter Victor.]

VICTOR—One month ago I was Victor Herndon, full of hope for years of happiness, but now they are all blighted. Yes, blighted, perhaps, forever. All hopes, all hopes have fled. Nothing seems visible now but death and disgrace., What am I in the eyes of the world? A murderer, murderer, murderer, and the people thirsting for my blood. They may have it if she will give the verdict of not guilty, *but* if she says guilty—that I cannot stand. [He is silent awhile.] Will she walk to-night? Lucy says she walks this grove. Surely the acronical moon will tempt her as it travels along its starry pathway, robing dull earth with a silvery mantle; but I, like a spirit, must vanish as it reaches the goal of day. O, Father, my Father, what have I done to displease Thee? [Enter Lucy.] Oh, heaven, defend me. [He falls upon the ground. Lucy starts toward him, but stops as he partly rises.] I must prove myself innocent; I must see Myra this night. I cannot bear to live while she believes me guilty. She cannot, she must not; I'll see her to-night. If she believes me innocent, then I will give myself to the law; but if not, I will die in her presence. [He rises and starts to leave the stage.] There—there she comes now. [He recoils and secretes. Enter Myra and walks up and down the stage very slowly, followed by Victor, but unobserved. Enter Florence, unobserved, and exits immediately.]

MYRA—O, what a poor unfortunate ceature I am. I am unhappy; yea, miserable. Why was I not left where I knew nothing but happiness? Why

was I brought here amid sorrow and affliction, and
to witness murder, and to die an untimely death?
Oh, Glenmore, Glenmore, my fortune for Glenmore.
[Glenmore, the asylum from which she was taken.]
O, Father, why did'st thou frown upon me in the
hours when I was so happy? Brighter days than
those never shown upon my young life, nor darker
days can never than these. I am a child of misfor-
tune. Would that I had died when I was an infant,
I would have been spared this hour; and yet there
is one to come that I cannot survive. They will
hang him I know, though he is innocent; and I am
accused as his accomplice in the murder of my dear
old uncle. [She weeps. Victor makes his presence
known.]

VICTOR —Myra, who says you are an accomplice
in the murder of your uncle? [She is frightened at
first at his appearance.]

MYRA—Leave me, leave me. How dare you ap-
proach me with your hands yet stained with my
uncle's blood? Leave me!

VICTOR—Murder! murder! two-fold murder!
How can I stand it? Oh, Myra, Myra, you cannot mean it. I who love you better than my life.
Fain would I have given my life a hundred times to
save you the sorrow of this hour. Oh! kill me if
you will; your sentence is death. I will leave you,
and that forever. [Starts to drink the poison.]

MYRA—Victor! Victor, you shall not. [Snatches
the vial.] I know you are innocent [She embraces
him.] Victor, they say you killed him.

VICTOR—Myra, how could you utter those words?

MYRA—I don't know, Victor; but tell me, how came your dagger to be the one that killed my uncle?

VICTOR—My dagger that killed him? [Springs from her.] Oh! the fiend! Who could have been so base? It's enough! I see it all! My dagger, Myra, I lost a week before the murder. My soul! it must have been—

MYRA—It must have been who, Victor?

VICTOR—No one, Myra, no one; I accuse no one; I will die first. [Enter John Hill and two others; Myra tries to shove him away.]

MYRA—Victor, fly. [He does not move.]

JOHN—Herndon, you are my prisoner.

VICTOR—Very well, sir; I will go.

MYRA—No, Victor, you shall not go.

JOHN—Miss, you must leave, or I will arrest you as his accomplice.

VICTOR—You lie; you will not, you base villian. [He rushes at him; John Hill draws a dagger; Victor catches his arm with one hand and his throat with the other; the two men rush to John's assistance; Myra jumps between one and Lucy the other with a knife.]

MYRA—Touch the innocent man if you dare.

LUCY—And I is guine stick dis here knife right through you. [Victor throws John Hill from him, and grabs Lucy's knife.]

VICTOR—Now, Hill, we are equal. [They fight;

Victor disarms him, and starts to kill him; Myra rushes between them.]

MYRA—Enough, Victor; spare him.

[Curtain falls a few moments, to change time.]

ACT SIX.

(Twelve months later.)

Scene I.—Same place. [Enter John Hill, dressed in the apparel of a ghost.]

JOHN—I wonder if she will come this way to-night. If she does, Victor Herndon nor any one else will save her. I will represent the ghost of Joshua Hill, and if I am not mistaken in the girl, she will swoon at his appearance, and I will administer this [pulls out a vial], which will send her to keep his company. He willed her all, and left me penniless; but I'll be rich before another day. [He looks to see if she is coming.] She comes. [He secretes. Enter Myra.]

MYRA—To-morrow, to-morrow, and Victor is no more. This night will I spend in prayer for him. It was in this grove where first I met him. It was in this grove where first he said he loved me. It was in this grove where we spent many happy hours together. It was here where I first knew he was innocent. O, Father! let him not suffer for the crime of another. [She hears a noise behind her; John Hill approaches; she looks back.]

What's that, a spectre? [He advances slowly.]
Could I laugh, I would. Times are desperate, but
not scary. I know that form; I have seen it before; it is not a phantom.

GHOST--Myra, I am thy uncle's ghost.

MYRA—If thou art my uncle's ghost, what say-
est thou.

GHOST—Why did'st thou lend a hand to slay
me?

MYRA—If thou art a ghost, why dost thy lie?
I will know thee better. Throw off thy disguise
or you shall die. [Draws a revolver and points it
at him.] Be quick, sir; I am in earnest. I know
your intentions, sir, are evil. Be quick. [He
throws off his disguise.] John Hill. Just as I
thought. This, sir, is your second attempt at my
life. Try it no more. Leave me! Your crimes
shall never be known. [Exit John Hill.] O, what
cruel times! what cruel times! My life is sought,
and for what cause I know not of, unless for the
mammon of unrighteousness. He and Florence
are my cousins, and the next heirs to Uncle Josh's
estate, which I now hold. Poor, wicked souls!
Before the setting of another sun they will be the
rightful heirs to his estate, for I will be no more.
[Enter Florence, walking in her sleep.] Florence!
What brings her here? His reprieve! his reprieve!
[She runs to meet her.] No; she is asleep. Surely,
she must be. [She touches her arm and tries to
wake her.]

FLORENCE—[Still asleep]: Let me go. I did not do it; I did not. Let me go. It was he.

MYRA—What can be the matter? Florence, awake, awake. Why are you walking here asleep? Do you know it is dangerous? [She awakes.]

FLORENCE—[She catches Myra around the neck, then springs from her.] What right have you in my room, Myra Gramer? Your intentions are evil. Leave me this instant. You breathe the air of wickedness. Go! Leave me, and hide your guilty soul in the waters of the James. Go! It is your name that gives you liberty.

MYRA—I will leave you, but only to rid myself of evil company. But remember, the soil upon which you stand is mine. No words from you can harm me now. But mark me well, Florence, that the terms upon which you say I am spared may be yours. [Exit Myra.]

FLORENCE—[Bewildered]: Myra! Myra! come back; come back. Spare me! spare me! O, did I dream aloud? O, my head, my head! Where am I? Where am I? I never was here before. I know not the place. I thought I was in my room. Kate! Kate! No; here are trees; here is ground. Myra! Myra! come back. I know not which way to go. How came I here? Am I—can I be in hell? I feel as if I were—I were suffocating. The air smells sulphureous. Oh, Victor! forgive me. [John Hill passes through the grove some distance from her.] Oh! what is that? [She starts first one

way and then the other, to leave the stage. Enter
Catherine, Florence's servant.]

CATH.—Miss Florence! Miss Florence! what is
de matter? I has looked eberywhar for you.

FLORENCE—Oh, Catherine! Catherine! did you
see it? Did you see it?

CATH.—See what, Miss Florence?

FLORENCE—A ghost.

CATH.—No, Miss Florence, I didn't seed anything
like dat. I spek you seed me when I was looking
for you. Ha! ha! ha! dat will do; I looks like.a
ghost.

FLORENCE—Catherine, take me from this place.

CATH.—Follow me, den, Miss Florence; I know
de way. [Exit both. Scene closes.]

*Scene II.—Three o'clock in the morning. Myra's
room.* [Myra asleep on a divan. Enter Diana.]

DIANA—Something guine wrong round here; my
mind tells me so. Here 'tis three o'clock in de
morning and I ain't closed dese eyes. [She goes
to Myra's bed and finds her not there.] Hi! whar
Miss Myra; whar she? [She looks around and
finds her on the divan.] Here she is, poor honey;
hasn't gone to bed yet. Miss Myra—poor child,
she's sleep without a bit of kiver on her. [Gets a
blanket and throws over her.] Ah, dese is dreadful times, dreadful times; but nobody is guine harm
dis child while dis old nigger is here. I is guine
stay right here 'till she wakes. What's dis here?
[Finds her revolver.] A pistol. Dis is de right

thing for dese times, I tell you, child. I 'spician something, and spician somebody. Dey is guine hang Massa Victor, but he didn't kill Massa Josh, and de same one dat had a hand in dat, is guine harm dis child. Dis nigger ain't no fool. So I is guine watch dis child. I is—hush! hush! I hears some one coming; I is guine hide and see who 'tis. [Takes the revolver and secretes. Enter Florence.]

FLORENCE—Asleep; yes, and thou shalt sleep forever; the dead tell no tales. You have heard too much to live; so inhale this sweet perfume and die. [She advances to her bed.] Not here! Ah, there. [She creeps to her side and takes from her bosom a vial.] Smell and die.

DIANA—[Steps in front of her with a drawn revolver.] Not to-night.

FLORENCE—Take this, and let it still your tongue. [Hands money to Diana.]

DIANA—Leave dis place, dat's all I ax you. [Florence walks backwards off the stage. Scene closes.]

Scene III.—[Myra in the woods reading Victor's farewell letter.]

MYRA—[Reading]: Dearest of all, when this, my final farewell, reaches you, perhaps I'll be no more. Grieve not for me; I know what you have suffered on my account. It is *God's will* that I should die for the crime of another; he knows that I am innocent, and you believe me so. I have no fear of death. Let the world believe as it will; so you believe me innocent, I can die without a pang. The day will soon come when I will be forgotten. Farewell, Myra, until we meet again in a better world.

Myra—O, why was I born to see this day—a day of injustice? Had I not been born, Victor would this day be free. Oh! say not, Victor, farewell, for I will accompany thee. The same vial with which thou did'st attempt thy life shall end my misery. Victor, Victor! I come. [Starts to drink, but hears some one coming.] What! Some one coming to disturb my last hour? Who can it be, that comes to this lonely spot? I will abscond. [She absconds. Enter Florence Hill and Charlie Crane.]

Myra—[Aside]: There; I see it all. He is the murderer.

Chas.—Florence, you scheme acted splendid. But Herndon, poor fellow, I feel sorry for him. I wish it was some one else; but he is better prepared to die than I am, so let him go. When do you intend to fulfill your promise, Florence?

Myra—[Aside]: Oh! can I not save him? [She looks at her watch.] I have but one hour. He shall not die.]

Florence—O, never mind the promise. We will see to that in the future. Herndon is not dead yet.

Chas.—No, he is not dead; he has an hour yet to live.

Florence—Yes; but should the secret be known in this hour, what would become of you?

MYRA—[Aside.] It shall be known. [She wrings her hands, and looks at her watch.] Will they never go?]

CHAS.—Yes, and what will become of you?

FLORENCE—You killed him; I did not.

CHAS.—Yes; you planned, and I executed; and, as the old saying is, you are as deep in the mud as I am in the mire.

FLORENCE—No; I am not.

CHAS.—Ha! ha! ha! you grow weak; never mind, the debt will soon be paid. [They hear some one whistling.]

FLORENCE—Hush; someone is coming; let's go. [They leave for other parts of the woods. Enter Paul; Myra runs to meet him.]

MYRA—Paul! Paul! bring me Grace, bridled and saddled, to the big oak! lose not a moment! Fly! fifty minutes, and all is lost! [Exit Myra. Scene closes.]

Scene IV.—Michaux's Ferry. [Enter ferryman.]

FERRYMAN—No crossing here to-day; water is too high. The James is furious, and she is still rising. [Enter Myra.]

MYRA—Ferryman! ferryman! take me across! quick! quick!

FERRYMAN—Not to-day, Miss; not to-day; water is too high.

MYRA—Ferryman! ferryman! say not so! I am in haste—be quick! I'll give you a hundred—I'll give you a thousand—take me across!

F. MAN—It would do me no good, Miss; we would be washed away.

MYRA—Then, I will go if I sink. [She plunges into the river.]   Scene closes.

Scene V.—People on the way to the hanging.

Scene VI.—Victor on the gallows.   [Enter Bill Robertson, a rough old farmer.]

BILL R.—Stand aside here; stand aside, and let me see it well done; make a good job, John, or let me tie the knot.   .

SHERIFF—All right, Robertson, you may tie the knot.

ROBERTSON—Helloo! he is quite willing. [Sheriff reads the death-warrant.]

SHERIFF—Victor Herndon, have you anything to say?

VICTOR—Only a few words, sir. Gentlemen, I am standing upon the verge of the grave, only a few moments to say farewell to the world. I have no hope for life now; no one can save me, although I am an innocent man. I do not dread death, but its the disgrace of the death I am compelled to die. I stand under sentence of the law for the crime of another, but it is my fate, and I have become reconciled. Gentlemen, I am accused of the murder of Joshua Hill, a man whose life I fain would have died to defend. I had no cause to kill him, but upon his life depended my future happiness. I went to ask him to promote my happiness by giving me the hand of his niece, when I found my own knife pierced into his heart. How could they accuse me of murdering Joshua Hill, a man whom I loved; a man who has saved my life more than once? The fiend who did the act aimed well, for he pierced his very heart. I have provided in my will two thousand dollars for the one that will bring to justice the true murderer of Joshua Hill. I am through; do your duty!

SHERIFF—Herndon I pity you, I believe you are an innocent man. It grieves me beyond expression, that it is my duty to perform this act of the law upon you. Robertson you can tie the knot, if you will.

ROBERTSON—But I don't *will;* you can tie *your* own knots.

SHERIFF—I will give twenty dollars to any man who will tie the not, and pull the trap.

FARMER—I'll tie it. [Starts to mount the scaffold.]

ROBERTSON—No you won't. [Jerks him down.] I'll kick this foot clear through you, you scoundrel. [While they are talking, the sheriff ties the not, pulls the cap, and is about to pull the string, when Robertson spies him.] Neither shall you, sheriff. [Levels his revolver at him.]

SHERIFF—Robertson, you are interfering with the law.

ROBERTSON—I care not. Conscience is my law, and my revolver will execute its judgment; and if you pull that string, somebody will have to hang me, and that won't be you. That lad is innocent, and he shall not be hanged. [The crowd shouts no! no! They hear a faint voice in the distance.]

MYRA—Wait! wait! wait! [Enter Myra. Gentlemen, he is not guilty]

ROBERTSON—My soul! what is it? An angel that confirms my opinion.

MYRA—Gentlemen, the murderer of my uncle is Charlie Crane. He is now on West View farm. I heard him confess the crime. I left him there three-quarters of an hour ago.

VICTOR—My soul! *that's* Myra. Remove this cap. [She mounts the scaffold. Loud cries of release him.]

MYRA—Victor, you are free. [She clasps him around the neck.]

ROBERTSON—I'll have him, if I have to swim the river.

SHERIFF—So will I. [Cuts the ropes from Victor. Deputy, look to the prisoner until I return. Look, Herndon, the maiden swam the river.]

MYRA—Yes, the ferryman would not bring me across; but Grace knew my errand and brought me safely across.

ROBERTSON—Hurrah! for the Maiden's Adventure. [Scene closes.]

Scene VII.—Woods at West View. Florence and Charlie alone.

CHAS.—Well, Florence, the tragedy is over, and Herndon is no more.

FLORENCE—What does it matter? I have no

sympathy for him, but I have my revenge. I leave this place to-morrow, never to return again.

CHAS.—Where will you go, dearest? [She frowns.]

FLORENCE—I know not where.

CHAS.—What about your promise?

FLORENCE—O, never mind the promise.

CHAS.—But you promised to be my wife.

FLORENCE—O, promises are made to be broken. I denounce them all.

CHAS.—Then I must have the fifty thousand.

FLORENCE—Fifty thousand! You are very lenient. If you want fifty thousand, you must seek it elsewhere. On the highway, perhaps, you will find it.

CHAS.—Florence, I am in earnest. I am ruined, and I must have your money. If you refuse I will accuse you of the murder to the law.

FLORENCE—What do I care for that? I can do the same. [Enter Paul with a gun.]

PAUL—[Aside]: I is tired of watching dese folks. I is guine make myself known. I is guine 'pear 'fore 'em, and if he run, I is guine 'bay Miss Myra's orders. I is guine shoot. [Steps before them; they rise from their seat, but sit down after seeing who it is.] Sarvant, Missus? [Bows low.]

CHAS.—What are you hunting?

PAUL—Jail birds, sar.

CHAS—Why, you mean jay birds.

PAUL—No, sar; I means jail birds.

CHAS.—Well, change your hunting ground; you won't kill any around here.

PAUL—I don' know, sar, 'bout dat. I ain't guine fur. If dey fly, run, or walk, I is guine shoot.

CHAS.—Florence, what does the fool mean? [Paul walks a few steps.] Look, Florence! What means this? [They see Robertson and the sheriff coming.]

FLORENCE—Fly for your life! It is the sheriff. [He starts to leave; Paul confronts him with his gun.]

PAUL—My missus told me to shoot you if you run, and I is guine do dat, sure.

[Enter sheriff and Robertson.]

SHERIFF—Crane, you are my prisoner.

CHAS.—For what am I your prisoner?

SHERIFF—For the murder of Joshua Hill.

ROBERTSON—And you have just long enough to live to get to the gallows.

CHAS.—I will go, but not alone. There stands my accomplice. [Points his finger at Florence.]

FLORENCE—I will not go. I die first. [She stabs herself, and presents a short scene of death, as the curtain slowly falls.]